CW00867942

FACES IN THE CONGREGATION

A Novel By

RICHARD D. BEARD

WESTBOW
PRESS®
A DIVISION OF THOMAS NELSON
& ZONDERVAN

Copyright © 2020 Richard D. Beard.

All rights reserved. No part of this book may be used or reproduced by any means, graphic, electronic, or mechanical, including photocopying, recording, taping or by any information storage retrieval system without the written permission of the author except in the case of brief quotations embodied in critical articles and reviews.

This is a work of fiction. All of the characters, names, incidents, organizations, and dialogue in this novel are either the products of the author's imagination or are used fictitiously.

WestBow Press books may be ordered through booksellers or by contacting:

WestBow Press
A Division of Thomas Nelson & Zondervan
1663 Liberty Drive
Bloomington, IN 47403
www.westbowpress.com
1 (866) 928-1240

Because of the dynamic nature of the Internet, any web addresses or links contained in this book may have changed since publication and may no longer be valid. The views expressed in this work are solely those of the author and do not necessarily reflect the views of the publisher, and the publisher hereby disclaims any responsibility for them.

Any people depicted in stock imagery provided by Getty Images are models, and such images are being used for illustrative purposes only.
Certain stock imagery © Getty Images.

Scripture taken from the New King James Version®. Copyright © 1982 by Thomas Nelson. Used by permission. All rights reserved.

ISBN: 978-1-9736-8041-3 (sc)
ISBN: 978-1-9736-8040-6 (hc)
ISBN: 978-1-9736-8042-0 (e)

Library of Congress Control Number: 2019919736

Print information available on the last page.

WestBow Press rev. date: 01/07/2020

Dedicated to Carolyn, the love of my life, always the prettiest face in the congregation.

Recently I returned to my home city. The job that took me away when my kids were still in school now brought me back temporarily. I had been back before, but I had never returned to the old church, or at least what's left of it.

All that remains is the Education Wing, and it is boarded up and surrounded by a chain-link fence. Where the sanctuary used to stand now is a charred heap of rock and muddy slime. Vandals had burned it down.

It is cold, rainy November. The mature bare trees seem to stand around in disbelief. Framed by the gray wool sky they seem to spread their arms in exasperation as if pleading for the return of the crowds, the joyous weddings, happy music echoing out of the open windows on warm Sunday nights, even for children to climb on them again.

The chain-link fence looks so menacing with the cold raindrops on it, and the sign about trespassers being prosecuted seems ironic when I think about all the ways the old folks used to try to get people to come onto this place. As I looked through the wire I realized that I couldn't even walk around in there; the cold fence became a border blocking me from returning not only to the site, but so it seemed to a better time. It was a time when church people called each other "brother" and "sister", when people had time to kneel in their pews, when they led the singing by waving their hands as the pianist played, before the use of accompaniment tapes.

Some trusting pioneers built this church up and it became a thriving worship center, a proving ground for several young bucks who went on to be big shots in the denomination. People in the neighborhood used to hear Harley Chapman's trombone playing "Joy Unspeakable" and other such tunes through the open windows on Sunday nights, but as far as I know, there were never any complaints. I used to watch from the front steps of the church as the world rolled through the four way stop while the adults clustered on the lawn after a service. I have technicolor memories of this place, but on this gray day it is stark black and white.

This neighborhood lies in disrepair, many homes abandoned, but that's not how it was in the early '50s when I stumbled on the scene. The area was to our city what Bailey Park was to Bedford Falls; under-priced little bungalows on rows of uniform streets with pine trees on the lawns. People were proud of their knotty pine "rathskellers", and there were good jobs to be had at the defense plant and the car assembly plant.

In the mid '60s I began to hear talk about the neighborhood "going downhill". Following the usual political upheaval, the Board finally succeeded in moving the church way out to the West County, almost all the way to the river. Some went along, some did not. New people came, some stayed, some left, others came and left, some died, some had children, and I drifted out of town with my job.

Now shivering I get back in my rental car. As I lock the door, I look cautiously around and behind me. This is now a dangerous area with news stories of drug deals and shootings. Looking through the beads on the window, I was stunned by what the trees and fence had told me.

The evil one began his taunting by suggesting that this is the end result of men's efforts to build churches, but I remembered the good times enjoyed here. As the years unfolded before my eyes I began to imagine how the reporters must have felt as they came upon the carnage and suffering at Gettysburg just after the battle.

I began to see the faces in the congregation that I had known over the years at this place. I began to hear their voices, some from the present, many from other times over the past forty years or so. Some spoke about others, some about themselves.

Awe-struck and bewildered by what I saw and heard, I seemed to gain a new perspective, but then, was it a new perspective? Or, was it just a new searching to know more about the heart and mind of God himself? Because you see, the faces in the congregation told me that many people who genuinely search for God gather in places such as this place used to be. But God, for whatever reason, allows lackeys from the dark domain, that murky demonic realm, to gather here too. These legions of demons use circumstances, relationships, rumors and even the utterances of well meaning but misguided believers to try to block our seeing and hearing about the real God. Some are victims of this, but those who genuinely search for God find Him in spite of it all. It seemed to me that Satan's army released all of its force against this place, but that the amazing grace of the Creating Father overcame it anyway in unexpected ways, over a long period of time, through unexplainable events and happenings that the old trusting pioneers might not have understood if they were still around. I included names when I knew them, but mostly I just tried to report what I heard and remembered.

At least, that is how I came away feeling, and in the pages that follow, I have reported as much as I can remember. You may arrive at a different conclusion after you hear from the faces in the congregation. I can only say that, in spite of all that I saw and heard, it is hard to deny the Amazing Grace that the songwriter wrote about.

Also there is an Epilog from the dark domain that they used to sing about; You know, the one the "He Arose" the victor from. I heard from one of the lackeys of the evil one. I wondered whether to even report what it said, considering that its' mentor is a liar and deceiver. I decided that you should make up your own mind about that too.

A Message to Edgar Lee Masters

For about two years, we shared earth's air, and then you died.

I never thanked my high school English teacher for pointing me in your direction. I found your work haunting, riveting and eerie, but only as my years go by do I fully get it.

Poems and Satires, Children of the Marketplace, and most of all, the Spoon River Anthology. No wonder you caused such a stir. They say that you used the real names of people in your Illinois town and got in some hot water for that. Your writings were part of what started my journey from being a naïve young high school junior to becoming hopefully, an alert, skeptical, aware young man.

In this writing I use fictitious names randomly chosen. Any resemblance to real people is purely a coincidence.

So, my distant friend, part lawyer, part writer, thanks for the inspiration, though you yourself borrowed the theme from Greek anthology.

To introduce myself to you and the Reader, on the next page I will write my own posthumous epithet, Spoon River style.

RICHARD BEARD

I drifted into manhood clueless and without much sense of direction. Then I met Carolyn. We were married and had two sons and five wonderful grandchildren. We faced life's struggles for more that 50 years.

And then, in what seems the blink of an eye, I found myself here.

To my sons and grandkids I must say beware, you live in a culture bent on self-destruction. So-called Social Media has been the spark that has ignited the powder keg of rebellion, apostasy, unrest, and irresponsibility. It is shaking the very foundation of the values that have made our society great.

I fear that when the keg burns out you will live in a lesser world.

But take heart, our Creator will still care. New steeples will rise, songs will still be sung, and God will provide good men and women to lead the way, He always has. When Paul wrote at Ephesians 5:29 about 'husbands love your wives" he wasn't just whistling Dixie when he said *"For no one ever hated his own flesh, but nourishes and cherishes it, just as the Lord does the Church"*.

So I hope that you find a place where people gather to discover our Creator. A place where, in your spirit, you can feel the presence of Him.

Just pick your friends wisely. Just be aware that not everyone else there is also seeking God, some have other motives.

JACK WHALEN

It was a big square brick building in an old neighborhood in the middle of town. You came out the door, down the steps, and right out onto the sidewalk. It had a small strip of a lawn with the usual sign. Traffic rumbled by.

Inside, a balcony hovered over two sides, and those who sat under it peeked around metal poles to see the pulpit. One wall had big windows, the only source of sunlight. The fourth wall was just plain bricks, floor to ceiling. There was the usual "vestibule" and the dark heavy pews. It always had that church smell.

In my days there, it was used by the frozen chosen; you know, the dignified, "high church" crowd. No hankie waving or hands lifted, reserved singing and dignity at all times. I felt OK with that.

But then a strange thing happened. The frozen chosen bought land out on the fringe of town, they built their version of the crystal cathedral and vacated the old square brick church. It sat abandoned for a long time. On a rainy day it almost looked like the windows wept with loneliness.

Then in came a new bunch along with their drums, keyboards, electric guitars and that old place started to rock. Many of the frozen chosen might have been appalled by the praying out loud, all that singing, the hand clapping, and especially the hugging.

First John 4:1 tells us to test the spirits, and I, for one, believe that a Spirit lives in that place. He was pleased when the frozen chosen, in their way, testified that Jesus in Lord, he is just as pleased when the new bunch, in their way, testifies the same thing.

And so, I don't think that God is bothered by differences in culture, customs, race, and worship, as much as most of us are.

RICHARD BELLINGHAM

In Proverbs 6 we read:

> There are six things the LORD hates, seven that are
> detestable to him:
>> haughty eyes,
>> a lying tongue,
>> hands that shed innocent blood,
>> a heart that devises wicked schemes,
>> feet that are quick to rush into evil,
>> a false witness who pours out lies
>> and a person who stirs up conflict in the community.

I know that we are not supposed to add or take away from what the Bible says, but I wonder if the writer was around today if he, or she, might add some more things. Maybe God doesn't detest all of these, but I bet they make his heart ache:

Gossip

> Parents dumping kids off and using Sunday school as
> free daycare
>> Business people showing up just to get business
> contacts

Those who feel their presence is a gift to the congregation

Those who come looking for faults of others

Those who feel it is their duty to evaluate the preacher for the benefit of others

Those who sing and perform for the benefit of their own ego only

Men who come to ogle women from behind

BEN BARONE

I heard that they call me Bickering Ben. That is the thanks I get for trying my best to be a good member and to improve things around here.

I put a lot of money in the building fund only to see the neighborhood rabble defile this place with their presence. The pretty new carpeting got worn down. All the fresh wall painting got scuffed up with fingerprints of the annoying little urchins.

I have never seen anything like these younger people; you can't tell anybody that they are wrong and offer corrective advice without hurting their feelings. When I was a young man I always wore a tie to church like you are supposed to, and I respected my elders when they gave me advice.

Seems to me the whole world has gone crazy.

DON HAGSTROM

A smokestack on the horizon puffs its white steamy
smoke
    Like a cotton trail against the blue turquoise sky
    The cornfields spread themselves proudly for the
inspection of the passersby
    Their horizontal rows wave and say, "Look how
well we are doing"

    Here a bridge, there an overpass, a tractor on an
access road, a semi flies by
    And soon out over the right front fender the skyline
of Chicago.
    Still 35 miles away, opaque against the misty sky,
like flake-board scenery from a play
    Imagine all that exists from here to there.

Though they are but yards apart, how different look the northbound
lanes from the south.

Northbound, Chicago awaits, where Babe Ruth swatted and Al
Capone crimed. Canyons of stunning beauty old and new, of concrete
and glass, marble and steel.

Southbound, back home and the life of a church board member,
and Bickering Ben.

Ben had two favorite expressions, one was that we do it like that because that is always how we did it, and the other was, we can't do that because we have never done that before.

I saw a silly Grouch Marx movie once where Groucho sang:

> I don't know what they have to say
> It makes no difference any way
> Whatever it is, I'm against it

And I thought of Ben.

Seth Blankenship

After that awful crash and during the long rehab I felt so much pain and frustration. I was very angry at the drunk that hit me and I wanted my pound of flesh.

I began to feel a bit like Job who said in Job 3:11

"Why did I not die at birth?
Why did I not perish when I came from the womb?"

I got so much profound Biblical counsel, mostly from people who had never been through anything like this.

Bill Emerick was all over me, once I faked being asleep when I heard him coming down the hall. Much like Job's so-called friends he would come in and say that I needed to pray more, seek the favor of the Almighty, and then God would restore me. Bill's theme was "you reap what you sew". Once he even said that God exacts less of us than our guilt deserves.

Preacher Boston came to see me a lot, and he would talk sports and stuff in general. He would always share a really corny joke.

And he always said two things: "I am praying for you" and "Do you need anything?".

BILL EMERICK

I used to see myself as the one who could explain scripture. I thought that I could restate it in terms that people would understand. I thought I had a special gift of explaining and clarifying passages that were hard to understand. I even thought I was the one that could settle all confusions and misunderstandings. I thought that if I had to sort of re-write places in the Bible that I was doing both God and others a favor.

Then one Sunday night Harley Chapman gave a talk about Saul who deviated from Gods' plan and justified it with sacrifices. He also mentioned the story found in 2 Kings about Naaman who wanted to receive God's blessing on his terms, not God's.

In his easy going style he concluded that "simple obedience trumps great sacrifices".

That night I began to change. It occurred to me, finally, that the Word had been around, and would be around, a lot longer than me. I even thought that perhaps it was not my place to change it. I told some of my friends at church about my change of feelings.

As time went by I noticed that people seemed more comfortable around me.

LLOYD BARON

What a craze this is! The CB radio; everybody has one. They call it the 12 volt Shakespeare, there are ditties on the radio, people brag because theirs has more range and power than yours. They talk about it in the foyer after church, and at all the Sunday school parties.

Truckers who stay cooped up in those cabs for long hours now have a window to the outside world. This seems like the ultimate electronic gadget to me, how will they ever top this in our lifetime?

All the truckers go to channel 19, where they jabber like so many magpies in a tree. At work they say stay away from channel 6, that is where the gays go. 9 is for Christians, 21 for law enforcement, and on and on.

It is good to know that everything that comes along draws lines and causes people to divide each other into groups.

It is not just "church people" who do this.

Nettie the Naz

At the shop we called her Nettie the Naz. That is because she went to the little Nazarene Church out on the highway just south of town. She was in our shop just about every week. She bought flowers for people in the hospital, flowers for the altar at her church, and flowers for the gravesites that she was going to visit.

She talked about her little church with a serene confidence and pride that appealed to me even though I was a Board Member at the big wealthy Methodist Church here in town. She let us know of her church loyalty in a way that did not make any of us want to push back. It was humble and encouraging and caused me to reflect on how I talked about my church affiliation to customers, friends, and suppliers.

Unwittingly she was my informant about stuff going on around town and I made a lot of money off of her without her even considering that, because her focus was elsewhere.

Not just for that reason, but when I heard that she was in the shop I always came out from the office to see her because there was this calming wisdom in her demeanor and in her voice. She had shared with me how she lost her husband, a combat Vet from WW2, and she beamed about her son the Veterinarian and his wife. I bragged on them for taking care of our puppy.

Then one day a nice young guy named Hugh walked in and said that he wanted to buy flowers for Nettie. He confirmed my worst assumption. Struggling with this news and with my angst about the lost revenue going forward, I stammered that Nettie was one of the wisest ladies that I had ever known. As I suspected, Hugh was her Pastor and, with a big smile, he stunned me with words that have since changed my life:

"Just imagine all of the things that she knows now"

PAUL HOGARTH

Karen's mother never liked me. Gerald was her pick for Karen. Even at our wedding reception she had a sour face and hovered over Karen like a protective hen. All she had for me were direct orders, like "Go thank the preacher" and "straighten your tie".

Only after she died did I learn that she had gone to Reverend Boston and told him that I was bad for Karen. She tried to enlist his help in getting us to split up; she asked him to counsel Karen about us.

Boston would have none of it. Now I understand why Karen's mother was always one of the preachers' biggest critics.

BART WATSON

One Sunday night they were short one usher. Harley asked me to "jump in" and help with communion. I panicked, imagine, me of all people, serving communion. To me it seemed that some were reluctant to take the bread and wine from me, saying with their body English that it didn't really count as communion. It was as if films were being shown on the wall of all the silly things I had done. I think that I flushed with embarrassment, and I felt so unworthy to be doing that. And I hoped that God wasn't going to get mad at me.

Later I talked to Harley about it. He gave me that patented laugh and with a big toothy smile he said "You are right!". I couldn't believe it, especially when he went on to say that he wasn't worthy, Rev. Boston wasn't worthy, not even Billy Graham or the Pope was worthy.

But then he said that we are all worthy because of the Blood of Jesus and he would be glad to tell me more. It wasn't so much what he said but by the peaceful confident way that he said it that stuck with me.

I should have took him up on his offer back then and maybe I wouldn't be in this mess now.

Jimmy Salerno

Otis Murphy was a devout man, so they all said. He referred to "The Catholic" and the same way that the bigots referred to "The Colored" in describing their perceived flaws and shortcomings.

Otis was convinced that "The Catholic" were the arch-enemy of Christianity and were by far the biggest threat around, and he spent much time whenever he could elaborating on his reasons. Mostly that it was all ritual and all they want is your money, so he said.

But he was so influential and respected around the church house I figured that he must be right. I begin to know some of The Catholic and after my initial wariness of them wore off, I began to see that we shared a common vision. It was a vision of a suffering Messiah, foretold by Prophets, who offered his blood for our indiscretions.

I have heard before that when a person comes out of a cult he needs to go through a period of "debriefing" to overcome the selfish teachings of greedy false prophets.

I wonder if it is the same for a person coming out of a church full of "devout" men.

Erin Grant

I heard your little indictment of Otis Murphy. I can't say that I disagree with you. But remember, it is easy to look at the faults of others and rationalize your own shortcomings. Who knows, had it not been for that icy road that night, Otis would have wised up over time like so many did.

He was a work in progress and God has his own timetable, you know.

Sure, he erred on the ultra-conservative side, but for every Otis there are countless guys who err the other way. He was loyal to his family and always did what he really thought was right. Can you say that?

Debriefing? Absolutely! But among those who need debriefed are plank-eyes like you and me.

ELLIS WILLIS

Attendance had been dropping. In open board session not much was said about the cause. Privately though, there was plenty of finger pointing. Some blamed the music, some the preaching, some the color of the carpet.

Once I heard somebody say that a lumbering donkey is a sleek race horse designed by a church committee. Well, in this instance they decided the answer to slipping attendance was to have "dinner on the grounds". There was the usual contest about who could invite the most people.

The big day came and some new faces did show up. There was a handsome young couple with a pretty baby in a new car. They smacked of success and prosperity. There was a lonely looking older man, not too well dressed and appearing to have been jarred by life's storms. He seemed bewildered and lost and he had an odd smell about him. Then there were some neighbors with their children, some Hispanic, some Asian, some Black.

I will never forget dinner on the grounds.

I saw the church inner clique fawning over the young couple. Inviting them over and competing with each other for their attention.

I saw the old man walk down the sidewalk alone, after standing around for an hour or so.

I saw the looks that were given to the robust little kids from the neighborhood.

I heard how they were spoken to; the scowling tone of voice. I saw the parents prevent the church kids from playing with them.

I could tell you the conclusions I reached, what my resolutions were, and what changes happened in me.

But instead let me ask, how would you have felt?

Rodrigo Diaz

I am Rodrigo and I work at United Parcel Service. I used to live on this street when I was little. One day a plump little man with black glasses and a white shirt and a thin black tie knocked on our door. Mama thought that he was an insurance salesman, or worse.

He asked us to come the church on the corner Sunday for dinner. Mama didn't go but I walked up there. Wow! Fried chicken, corn, casseroles, cake, ice cream, games and lots of people. And there was Mr. Chapman, the man that came to our house. He had his big horn, and he took some of us kids in to see it. It was in the beautiful case with red velvet lining, and he played it for us! Most people there treated me the way I expected and I didn't know what to think about somebody like him being that nice to us. He would see me in the neighborhood and always ask me to come to church. He would say "come and stick with me" but I never did. I didn't have any Sunday clothes.

These days when the subject of God or Jesus comes up, I always think of that man. I wonder where he is, or if he is still alive. It makes me wish that I could find him.

MARLENE GOLDBAUM

Recently I had a dream that caused me to wake up in a cold sweat.

I dreamed that I had gone on an errand and left my house unlocked. When I returned I found that sinister, violent intruders had snuck in and were hiding in my house. The dream was terrifying as I went from room to room only to be attacked by these thugs, against whom I was hopeless.

The most unusual part was that I was trapped in my house and could not run outside and call for help. I remember thinking how stupid it was of me to leave the house unlocked.

After I woke up and settled down, I prayed. I confess that I don't always pray regularly, and sometimes only when I wake up in the middle of the night realizing that I need to. As I prayed, the dream took on a special meaning to me.

To me, just as we leave our door unlocked, so it is if we don't guard our heart from the evil thugs who attack it.

Sounds corny, I know. But just think about it.

James Plant

Mr. Edwards always used some kind of greasy concoction to slick his hair straight back. His reddish brown glasses and wide lapels were his trademark. He always had a distinctive smell about him, kind of mixture of Vitalis and mothballs. His wife always had a toothy, friendly smile and she always called him "Mister" in front of us kids.

He was my Sunday school teacher. He told us about his days as an army paratrooper and how scared he was, how they could not even light a match at night in case the enemy saw it. He used feltboards on easels with cotton camels, cardboard shepherds, and assorted props to illustrate Bible stories that kids learn. Daniel and the lion's den, Joseph and his coat and brothers, the Manger scene, temples, caravans, palm branches and false idols. He talked about Moses and Abraham, Isaac and Sarah as if he had once known them.

He was just a timekeeping clerk at a local brake pad assembly plant. He never seemed to be too involved in all the important stuff that went on at the church. When the men would caucus on the lawn he would be walking to his car. But he always stood ten feet tall in my mind.

You ask what great theological concepts did I learn from Mr. Edwards? You are missing the point.

It is easier to try to understand God the Father if you have an earthly father as a model. If your earthly father is gone, or in my case, (worse yet), there, it is much more difficult. At least I had a guy like Mr. Edwards. But to my shame, I don't think that I ever thanked him.

BILLY BARTON

Rev. Boston caused a big stink that morning. As he shared his sermon about Jesus feeding the 5,000, I looked around the sea of faces and I could his detractors getting fidgety. They couldn't wait for the sermon to end so they could get out to the lobby and breezeway and talk about it.

They said, "Imagine, questioning the very Bible itself like that".

Saying that 5,000 or more, that out of all of them, only one little boy would remember to pack lunch. Saying that just the presence of Jesus encouraged others to share and love. So those who brought food willingly shared it with strangers. How ridiculous!

Nope, only one kid brought food and Jesus did a magic trick, end of story, anything more is blasphemy!!

But later I heard Roscoe say that it was easy enough for Jesus to create more food, much more miraculous to change the callous hearts of the people there that day so they became willing to share food with strangers. Roscoe thought that was a much more incredible miracle that happened that day, and can happen these days. "What a larger view of Jesus" he would say.

So it seems to me that just as the Israelites had conflicts between the prophets and the Kings, so our old church had conflicts between some of the old "Saints" and the preachers.

CHRISTOPHER DEAN

Dear Habakkuk,

In our Bible study we read your little book. Some wondered why we weren't covering the big stuff: the Gospels, Proverbs, Genesis, Psalms, Paul's letters, and so on. Rev. Boston jokingly said that to find your book, we should go to Mathew, turn left and go back five lights. Yours seemed like a sort of an obscure little book out there in no mans' land.

But as for me, I like your work. You were really mad at God and you let him have it. He patiently let you lay it all out for His book. You scored big with "the righteous shall live by faith" and those five woes and that description about the "puffed up" evil one and that expression "as greedy as the grave". Still you put together one incredible finish to your little book. Scholars use the usual "little is known" about the author line in their commentaries. Your book reads like a Psalm, with musical instructions and all. In fact, if today's TV did a documentary on you it might be entitled "Psalms, the Lost Episodes".

And so I am dying to know:

How do you like the English translation?
What is shignioth, anyway?
Was Habakkuk your real name or a pen name?
What would you be called today?
How was your writing done, on parchment? Stone?

Where is the original manuscript?

When were you born?

What do you think about today's use of the "Watchtower" expression?

Where did you live?

Were you a man or a woman?

Were you a writer? A temple guy? A priest? A musician? Or just a person inspired by God to write one of what we call the books of the 'Minor Prophets"?

Did you write anything else?

Looking down from Heaven have you seen Harley Chapman and his work? Were you like him?

How long did it take you to write your book?

Did you know any of the other big writers of your day; Isaiah? Jeremiah? Amos?

What happened that led you to write to God "I have heard of your awesome deeds"?

What changed your attitude?

What do you think about today's music?

Would you have attended my church?

Is there anything that could have been done about the Boston situation?

Is what happened in our church to be expected?

Did you have situations like ours back in your day?

How much did you know about Jesus when you wrote your book?

Why do you suppose God left us with all these mysteries to wrestle with?

If you wrote your book today, would it start with the same bitter questioning? Would you arrive at the same awesome conclusion?

Sandy Skeen

Have you ever sat beside a road? Not a bustling interstate with its' two-way constant drone of truck tires and horns. Not a dirt road out in the country used once a week in good weather by its farmer-owner. No, not those, but have you ever sat by a two lane highway, perhaps waiting for help as your big sister's radiator steamed. Or maybe waiting for you mother to come out of the office, where she pleaded with some bespectacled nerd about welfare payments or school enrollment for you?

When you did, didn't you hear the sound of a passerby? First the hum in the distance alerted you that a vehicle was coming. Louder and louder. A truck? A rich guy in a Cadillac? A bus with your friends? An ambulance? The distant sound is full of hope, anticipation, and wonder about the future.

Oh, there it is, just a grey sedan, now passing by. And the sound of it changes.

And in a blink, its' engine and tires duet a refrain of farewell. Their plaintiff song pleads to the signs and bushes and horizon a chorus of regret for missed chances, things that might have been, choices made in error, and things that should have been said. Soon the last little murmur is heard, the sedan is over the horizon and out of sight.

So it was with some of the people who came to our church, passed through and then moved on.

Floyd Adams

Last week my wife sent me downstairs to pick up some papers. I don't like going up and down the stairs because of my knees, but neither does she.

They have children's Sunday School down there and it was bedlam. There was singing, piano music, crying, squawking, and all kinds of rattling and the patter of footsteps everywhere.

In the middle of it all in the hallway I ran into a little boy about 7. Without being asked he told me his name and asked mine. He showed me his crayon papers and told me of a new song they learned. I asked him if he liked his teacher and he said "Sure, she is swell!". In that moment it was as if I was looking not at the boy, but at a magic mirror that reflected myself at age 7, and that was a long, *long* time ago. Old feelings bubbled up; feelings of hope and wonder. I remembered how I loved to hear the stories of Jesus and Disciples, and pictures of Mary riding on a donkey, and rich stories of temples and idols, of lions dens and fiery furnaces vividly illustrated and told by some old enthusiastic believer, now long gone.

There are magic mirrors at church, seek them out.

PATTY PAULSON

Ed and Marlene were ramrods in our church. Whenever something needed to be done, they were there. Ed, a great singer and musician, was always able to organize a cantata or Holiday program of some sort. He ran the building program and got the money, drove the project home, ruffling a few feathers. Marlene was always there with a pie for a new family, or helping in the kitchen.

Tom and Janet were usually there on Sunday morning, but it seems like that was about it. They were always good friends of Ed and Marlene; they went to Sunday dinner together, and to the lake, things like that.

Tom's accident was tragic. And when Marlene announced her cancer, we could tell it would not be long for her.

Nobody has ever said anything to me, but I was always surprised at how fast Ed and Janet got married after words.

I can't help but wonder what they were thinking all those years.

Howard Rumping

When the Jennings couple came in I did everything I could. I shook their hand, I showed compassion.

Why we had to sing that old dirge "Jesus Calls Us" at a time like that is beyond me.

And Boston could have been more eloquent and upbeat, after all, we had guests in the crowd!

So you don't have me to blame because we can't get new members.

Jasper Jennings

We came to your church once after my ordeal. I must say the friendly handshakes and neutral questions reflected a warm, caring atmosphere. The people I met were very nice. All that happy music was encouraging, although I wondered when it would end. That one song stuck in my mind, "Jesus calls us o'er the tumult of our life's wild, restless sea". A catchy melody too. It seems that you people sang it just for me to confirm what I had been thinking.

The Senior Pastor seemed to care that we were there and he was friendly and approachable and made me and my wife both feel comfortable.

Somehow though, the spontaneous, unstructured sort of way things happened there just didn't feel right to us. And we found ourselves settled in a church with more liturgy and order, and even dignity. In that culture we have journeyed along seeking to know God better.

Still I thank you for your kindness. I thank your founders and I thank your eloquent minister and your innocuous music guy. You did, in one morning, wake up a longing in me to find our Father.

Edward Charlton

Howard was so tall, and he carried a big Bible that looked like a suitcase. With his hair slicked back and his three piece suits, even in the hot summer, he was a sight to see.

But on Sunday night after church, the clusters would form. Some behind the back row of pews, some out in the vestibule, and in the summer, out on the lawn. Some clustered to critique the sermon and the music, usually negative. Some to talk about their kids and problems. The men would cluster and talk about Corvettes and sports.

But Howard, who the other adults seemed to ignore, always drew a gaggle of kids. And he always baited us in with an attention grabbing question. Something like "Did you know that a man was once thrown into a pit with hungry lions, and did not get hurt?" Some kids continued to play tag on the lawn, but some, like me, wanted to know more. So he opened that big bible and showed full page black and white pictures and told the story with vivid illustrations and a confident passion that made, well, at least me, feel like I was right there. He must have been 7 feet tall but he always squatted like a baseball catcher to look at us while he told the story. The other thing about Howard, he always smelled like Old Spice, or Brylcreem or something, I heard people make fun of him because he put it on a little too strong.

My final thought about Howard is this: some people don't use a lot of perfume or after shave, some dab a little on, and some pour it on to excess until you feel smothered and want to get fresh air.

Some people don't share their feelings about God, some will sort of dab it on you a little and make you feel assured and confident, but a few will pour it on you with excess until you feel smothered and want to just get away.

I was eleven years old when Howard died, and I asked God why that had to happen, and after that I cried.

GERALD PATREDO

They lived above the "annex", the building owned by the church and next to it. Because his kids and I were pals, I spent time at their house usually before or after church. His wife was a shaker and do-er in the church, often a champion for the downtrodden.

That narrow parking lot seemed like a mysterious frontier to a separate world distinct from the sterile Church World. In the Church World the people smelled OK, they spoke politely about spiritual things, they were indeed religious but often detached somehow, too busy, too snobby, too sanctified.

But across the parking lot and up the stairs in the Netherworld, he sat in his recliner; the outcast. Always a warm greeting and questions about how it was going, always reeking of beer and slurring his words a bit. The tattered Bible on his end table always looked so out of place. But he had lots of funny stories and never a critical word about the church so near yet so distant across the asphalt frontier. Clearly he was not welcome there because of his choices.

Of all the people, Rev. Boston was the only one who never talked down to him. I was there a couple of times to hear the happy, laughter filled conversations that the two men had. Boston always listened to his rambling dissertations about God and Bible, and always offered a pleasant invitation to "come on over".

In the Church World he was a write-off, but in the Netherworld, only he and God know of his faith. After the liver disease took him down I was left wondering if intercessory prayers for him mattered at all. Twenty years after, I have concluded that they do matter, and the only question left is who they affect: him, me, or the denizens of Church World?

SEAN TUCKER

Every Sunday we went to church. My Dad drove the car. On a typical Sunday we would load into the car and soon Dad would be griping and complaining about this moron or that idiot in another car. I won't repeat some of the names he called those other drivers.

I began to notice that there was an invisible line, about 2 blocks in all directions from the church. As we crossed it my Dad changed. His voice got softer, his face became serene and his whole personality changed. It stayed that way all morning until we headed home.

Once we crossed the line something would always irritate him and out would come the vile arrogance of a hopeless, increasingly frustrated man. It was frightening at times.

I always wished that I could extend that magic line, all the way out to the edges of the world.

DELSIA WRIGHT

The last thing I remember about television was watching Red Skelton and Lucy on a round black and white tube.

I was surprised when they let me come back down just long enough to see what has changed in 44 years.

I was astonished at the big colorful screens and the sounds but I was flabbergasted though with what I saw!

Why the preoccupation with guns? Seems like it was bang bang bang all night long. I saw a couple of shows where a conflict developed but at the end of the show it was settled with a dramatic gunshot.

And the adultery and use of some of the language, my goodness!

Can anyone, even little children, see that now?

Do children growing up think that gunfire is the way to settle problems?

Everyone seems indifferent to the hours of slaughter on TV. How long has it been like this?

What went wrong? Did an evil bloodthirsty nation conquer our society?

How can you people just stand by and let this happen?

Jason Issert

I was canvassing the neighborhood with Harley and I argued with him about the sermon he preached the week before. Boston was on vacation. In the sermon Harley bragged on Jesus for turning water into wine at a wedding.

I said I just don't see no way that Jesus would create an alcoholic beverage. I was upset at the thought of it and I let him know. Harley, with his ever present peaceful smile said something about impure water back then and that things were different in a lot of ways.

He suggested that I missed the point. He thought that maybe because Jesus was invited to the event, he did a miracle and showed his control over nature. He also thought that Jesus showed one way that he can provide solutions to problems.

He said that in his private prayers he often thanks Jesus for the lives of people where Jesus "turned the wine back into water"; in Harleys' words, it is another way that Jesus provides solutions to problems.

It is taking me a long time to understand this.

AMY BERRINGER

I grew up in this Church, we got married here, my Dads' funeral was here, and I have so many memories, mostly good. But thinking back about the people and things that happened down through the years, it just seems that the Devil has an army of spirits whose job it is to distract and confuse the worshipers.

These evil beings are relentless and merciless and they use two main vehicles: relationships and circumstances.

Some days I don't want to think about that. Other days I can see how God and some believers prevail over this vile army.

NICKY HILTON

My best friend in junior high was Ira Feinstein. We didn't fit in with the tough guys on the school yard. Ira used to talk to me about how God rescued his people, in vivid detail.

I got the impression that it had just happened.

Once we were working on a project for school and Ira came to my house on a Saturday morning to help me work on it.

My Mom was cleaning up and she was sweeping the floor. She always sang as she swept and this day she was singing "I'm going to take a trip on the old Gospel Ship, and go sailing through the sky".

Ira was dumfounded. He had a sort of panicked look about him. I was embarrassed. He never said much about it except one time he said he thought my Mom was a little weird.

Later he invited me to a Seder at his house. His parents were much friendlier than what I was used to from adults. We went through the whole meal in great detail. At one point I asked Ira's dad why they don't believe in Jesus, and I might have had an accusing tone to my voice.

He answered that when he sees Christians offering food and comfort and charity to those in need, he can see Jesus in that, but it is so rare. I left their house that night with my tail between my legs.

The next day I said to Ira "and you think my Mom is weird?"

He thought for a minute and then with a scowling look said that maybe someday we will ride on that ship, but on different decks.

Ira is now a distinguished trial lawyer and we stay in touch, I see him at Chamber of Commerce meetings.

BILL WESTWOOD

Hockey has a rink
Baseball has a diamond
Football has a gridiron
Basketball has a court

The Church has a venue for games too, sometimes a sanctuary. Sometimes a fellowship hall, sometimes a classroom, sometimes a road game. Most games like Rook or Jinga are harmless and fun, other games are not so harmless:

Trash the Pastor
Manipulate the servants
Water the theology
Spread the venom

Unfortunately games like this do not have officials and umpires, or even consistent rules.

And the losers are other worshipers and the winner is <u>always</u> evil.

ALAN PERKINS

Many decades ago when I was only 9 years old, I went to church as usual with my parents. There was a special speaker, a tall red-haired man who came all the way from the General Headquarters.

He was a pleasant, gentle man, with funny things to say. But then he told a story about being 9 years old and feeling the voice of God and not really knowing what to do. He said that he went out in the woods and sheltered under a willow tree and prayed and the he felt the presence of God in his heart.

I went home that afternoon and I could not get that out of my mind, and so I prayed. From that day on I have felt the presence of God in my life and for the most part I have followed His guidance.

So for me, no willow tree, and I don't think I am that special. But I do think that speaker drove all the way from Kansas City, and all those people got up, got dressed, came to church and had a service just for me.

HAL GIBBONS

Some say Nicodemus came to Jesus at night because he didn't want anyone to see him. After all it might compromise his power in the Sanhedrin to be associated with this radical figure. I do wonder how many of us come to Jesus "in the night" for personal reasons.

Others say that night time was the best time to catch Jesus when he wasn't stampeded by crowds. I give old Nick the benefit of the doubt, at least he came to Jesus with his question. And like us, many times we take questions to Jesus day or night, and the answer isn't what we expected, or wanted to hear.

Nicodemus didn't get the point about being born again, asking how could he possibly crawl back into the womb.

Today, sometimes we don't get the point either. For many it is understood that being born again means suddenly getting heavenly gifts, like success, wealth, a private VIP hotline to God, the ability to speak in tongues, and the sudden entitlement to counsel everyone else around us. I am thinking of guys like young Bill Emerick.

Maybe that's why many sincere believers often don't want to be branded as born again?

Connie Sherbrooke

I loved Christmas at the church. The misty sanctuary with cardboard stars wrapped in tin foil. I loved the songs, so bright, perfect and pure. I loved the makeshift manger scene and the silly shepherd costumes. I loved all the smiles and what seemed like a break from all the conflict. Time stood still and I never felt so serene and safe as I did then. I never wanted to leave.

But then it was back out the front door into the glare, a wheezing bus rolls by and reality returns. And I found myself back in a loud unpleasant world where a president can get shot and communism can spread.

TOM TROUTMAN

In high school I had a girl friend named Maria. She took me to her house once and her father gave me the once over. He told me that he had a gun and a shovel and the he knew how to use both. I think he was kidding, because he quizzed me about my church affiliation and filled me in on his. He told me his daughter would not be allowed to change.

I snuck off to mass with her, and she snuck off to evening church with me, told her parents she was going to a dance. I would have needed a different excuse.

She liked the spontaneity of my church, I liked the discipline and dignity of hers.

As teenagers it was endless love until I got busy with baseball practice and she started hanging out with this blond guy from Australia.

ROBERT DEAN

Mr. Pelham was a prosperous builder. He built new homes and subdivisions in our town. He always had a shiny new Cadillac, and was dressed in the finest silk suits, hair all moosed up and he move with a kingly air. His wife always came as if on display, jewels and the finest new threads, even for Wednesday night prayer meeting.

People clustered around them, and when Pelham spoke, everybody got quiet. He was a man of influence around that church, for sure. He used to sit toward the front, and while the opening hymns were sung, he set with his checkbook out on his knee. As the choir sang, he would pompously write his check, well aware of the gallery of fans around him.

When I got to be 20 and studied accounting, they put me in the office counting offerings. I did it for several years. In all that time, the biggest check I ever saw from the old phony write was for $50, and that was at Christmas.

Allison McAllister

When I was a kid, I saw a cartoon. I don't remember much about it, but it had a flock of magpies in a tree, laughing and making fun at our hero. Was it Bugs, Daffy, Porky, or someone else? I don't remember. But as I came to church it seemed to me that we had our flock of mocking magpies there. I suppose every church does.

Let me give you an example. Soon after Reverend Boston came here, in one of his early sermons, he said how unworthy he was to be a minister, and but by the grace of God himself he would probably be in jail, or maybe rehab somewhere. He said he had nothing of his own, but that any success he had was from God Himself.

One thing I have noticed about the mocking magpies, they flock together and smirk as they ask questions:

I wonder what he did in his past to make him say those things?

What makes him think he is qualified to lead us?

How can we get bread from him after what he said?

Did the district send him here because nobody else would take him, do we rate that low with the district, should we break away?

Hekyll and Jekyll were magpies you know.

MIKE PILLA

I just wanted to play ball. I was playing American Legion and I made the cut already for the basketball team in the fall, but there was something about that church league, fast pitch softball. It was Jackie Chapman that got my attention.

So I attended a few meetings and started to duck out, because I thought they were stupid, but Jackie stood up to me and said we don't care how good you are, if you don't come to church you can't play.

And I don't know how or when it happened but I just couldn't get those songs and those slogans out of my mind. Songs about the fountain, and all who come there lose all their guilty stains.

Now here I am in Seattle, minister to many, father to 5, still wondering if the old church house back there still stands.

JACKIE DAVENPORT

To me as a 12 year old, 17 year old Jackie Chapman seemed like a bully. He used to be such a nice guy, and play ball with us. But then he started pushing me aside to talk to the girls, and he was just a big show off.

Only after he died in Vietnam did they say that he was the one who kept inviting Mike Pilla to come play on the church softball team, but only if he attended Sunday School and Church.

Mike's story was a miracle, often I wondered whatever happened to him.

Jason Trammell

Harley Chapman taught me a lot about music and performing, especially with my trumpet. I know I got this job as the all night D.J. on the all request oldies station because of the little things he taught me.

But more than that, he taught me to focus on the promises found in the Bible. He sure could rattle those off even though he knew all the stuff going on.

Once when I was in high school we were driving home from the youth competition where I won a ribbon. We were listening to the station where I now work, and we put together this masterpiece. As usual, Harley laughed as only he could.

The Midnight Hour by Jason and Harley

How *Proud Mary* must have been of her *Angel Baby* whose *Whispering Hope* to all those who have *Nowhere to Run*, not even *Ahab the Arab* or *The Boy From New York City*. So *For What It's Worth*, come to *Where the Action Is*, and *Chances Are* you will find *Everlasting Love*, *If Only You Believe in Miracles*.....

Don't wait *'Til the Midnight Hour*, *Walk Don't Run* to the One ⁻*Who Wrote the Book of Love*, and *He'll make you Glad All Over* and show you the *Stairway to Heaven*.

In those days it was fashionable to be melancholy and share your burdens for the lost and the less fortunate. Harley did not play that game, he was always upbeat and talked a lot about blessings and promises. I was always impressed with what Harley said and how he said it. In hindsight I am now even more impressed with the things he didn't say, if you get my drift.

Louis Coleman

In 1961, some negroes came to our church on a Sunday night for the specific purpose of integrating our church. I say negroes because "Black", as the popular term, had not come into existence yet.

Because my mother was always there early, I heard through the office door a stormy, emergency Board meeting before the evening service, as soon as Pastor McCorkle got the phone call to say they were coming. Some wanted to stand at the door and complain they did not come to worship, but to use our church to make a political point.

McCorkle pleaded with the Board to do the right thing but he did not address how God loves all of his people. He didn't address it in his sermon either.

The Black people who showed up were well dressed, polite, and had a genuine interest in the preachers' scholarly discourse about Job. But after that night we never saw any of them again, to our discredit.

And rather than scorn those people, I was left wondering about all the other people who for years had come to church for reasons other than to worship but were given a warm welcome.

Eric Jackson

In the back of the church in the fall on 1960 I heard our preacher tell those clustered around that he was praying that Kennedy did not get elected: "The Catholic Church" would then take over in his view.

Here was a humble obedient servant who sacrificed so much. But maybe even utterances from saints have to be filtered by God before we hear them.

JOHN INGLAR

I played a lot of golf with Howard Rumping and I can't say that I ever like Reverend Boston either. Howard and I both thought that he was a little too friendly around the women. I never appreciated how he always walked to our car after church to greet us. He always wanted to greet Rosa from my side of the car and I think he wanted to see if her dress was riding up above her knees.

He always seemed so proud of himself and I thought that he always kissed up to the leaders in the church and the ones that he thought were the big givers.

I think that the things they say about him are true.

JACK BOSTON

I loved that flock and God gave me grace to at least try be their humble servant. Harley once told me that he was praying for my detractors but he never said who they were and I never asked. It is a challenging job with highs and lows. Many times I worked hard all week on a message and I was on fire about what I had to say, only to have the message received with indifferent yawns. Always though there were unexpected acts of kindness and reassurance, often from where I least expected them.

I always wanted to clear the air with people like John Inglar. John and Rosa always bolted out the back door right after a service and often I tried to catch them in the parking lot just to say hello and make a better connection with them both.

John was always adamant in finance committee meetings about my salary being too high. His gave his 16 year old son a brand new car for his birthday while I drove a six year old Chevy. I kept it clean and polished to keep up a good image.

Many times I wanted to lash out at John and Howard but God was kind to humble me and remind me that I was there for everyone. Most nights I could turn the matter over and even offer intercessory prayers for those guys. During those prayers I was always reminded that I should pray for Jack (me), that my focus and attitude needed correction because everything was normal.

On nights like that I could feel that I was where I should be and then I could sleep.

TERRY TAYLOR

During my junior year of high school the English Department put on a writing contest. Students were invited to submit an essay for the competition. I wrote a flowering, lovely piece about God, Church and Family. I thought it was wonderful and I began drafting my thank you speech in my mind.

As it turned out, the winner was a friendless loner that always carried a back pack and always dressed in military green. During Vietnam there was always a lot of that for sale at Goodwill.

The winning essay began by saying that while Cock Robin read Sartre, Jesus was led up the hill to his crucifixion. It was a compelling, accurate account of Jesus suffering and carrying his cross. It concluded with the words "I wish I had been there, to laugh".

The essay propelled the kid to instant popularity. And I thought that If you want attention, if you want your jokes laughed at, take cheap shots at God, and especially Jesus.

Hollywood sure understands that, don't they?

Sherman Fletcher

I did not like being uprooted and forced to move to a strange city because of my job. But it was my best option. It was hard on our two boys being pulled out of middle school and forced to start over in the middle of the school year. I had to travel more than I wanted and was gone a lot.

We went to a church nearby. The guy that ran the music was very talented and pleasant. The senior pastor always gave a scholarly thoughtful presentation.

But Wanda and I starting calling the place the "fortress of snobs". It seemed so hard to find friends our age, friends who could help us find our way around town and help us restore order to our disrupted lives.

There was one couple though, the Stricklands, who befriended us and showed a lot of interest in us. The husband asked me about my hopes and dreams for the future, and one Sunday they invited us over for lunch after church.

So we went.

They had a nice apartment and my younger son spilled his water at the table as we started lunch. We had a nice lunch with pleasant conversation and then we were invited into the living room. And then, like lightning, out came the easel and the Amway presentation started.

I have been told that I am "a little too transparent" at times, and I let feelings show. I told him half way through that we were new in town, did not have contacts and that, in any event, we were not interested.

During the car ride home we made up a song called "out pops the easel" to the tune of "pop goes the weasel".

Thereafter when we saw the Stricklands at church I always made a point to greet them and thank them for a great lunch. In return there was never more than a lukewarm handshake. But as time went by we made lots of friends.

We learned a lesson that human nature is such that you can't always jump into a strange new church and expect instant comfort. It takes time but it is always worth it.

Dennis Durand

I was trying to sell an insurance package to a big church. I put my best suit in the cleaners, I prepared a fancy package with a quote. I readied myself the best I could. I needed the money.

I showed up at the appointed time.

They led me back through the hall to the church office. I had not been in a church for a while, and had never been in this one. I was struck by that familiar smell though. Funny how all churches smell the same, regardless of the doctrine.

Along the way I saw, through the doorway, tiny little tables and a tiny little wooden chair in the room where they teach the preschoolers.

I felt my poise and composure slipping away.

I thought about the people who cared enough to teach us little people, and the future of the kids who came there Sunday mornings

I remembered chairs like that in my home church and how indifferent I was to them, even though I once occupied one. I thought about songs I learned there.

The senior pastor said "Are you OK?", and I replied "Sorry, just allergies I guess"

I walked out of there with a signed order, but the joy a successful salesman gets was overshadowed by a new resolve to get back to church and share the legacy of Mr. Edwards with those bright young minds in my own home church.

MARK NAPIER

Jerome was the czar of the big adult Sunday school class. The class wielded power when it came to important matters like adding on to the building. They were the in-crowd, made up mostly of the upper crust people.

Jerome always sang loud so everyone around him would know he was there. He always bellowed out a loud amen louder than the others. When the speaker said something funny the crowd gave a polite laugh, and after that died down but before the speaker spoke again Jerome would put his ha ha ha out there so everyone would hear it and know that he had pronounced approval on the joke.

It came to the attention of the Board that his class did not turn in their Sunday school collections like every other class. As it turned out Jerome's wife ran a travel agency and the class had its own treasury. It collected funds to get better discounts and the class went on "mission trips" to places like Nassau and Catalina Island. Separate records were kept for each member and every January Jerome issued contribution letters, using the church tax ID, for donations made that were used for those private trips.

As a retired IRS agent I was adamant that this practice should stop. Reverend Boston agreed, and a couple of days later a got an angry phone call from Jerome. He was very condescending and he told me, among other things, that this was none of my business. I quoted him statue law, underlying regulations, private letter rulings and court cases and he said that I was naïve and that I should get in touch with the real world and that I should stop being a "stickler. He said there is no harm done and that this is the way to get things done.

I replied that this was tantamount to saying "it was just me and her, no harm done, she got paid and it is nobody's business".

Jerome hung up on me and we haven't spoken since.

JASON RITTER

What I saw over the years is that most people go through the ups and downs of lie and many acquire, over time, an understanding of God through studying the Bible, observing others, and by feelings inside their own spirit.

But not old Schuyler. He always spoke about himself in superlatives. He fancied himself to be a modern day Paul.

He always said in his younger days he was the most vile sinner "ever to walk the face of the earth". He once said that one day as he was walking the Appalachian Trail looking for songs, God knocked him down, the sky flashed and he heard the voice of God calling him to a special place in the Kingdom. (All his words)

I walked into McDonalds once and saw his wife sitting at an empty table. There he was at the counter with a line 5 deep behind him. He had a half-eaten Egg McMuffin and he told the manager it was soggy and he wanted another one, "And I want one for my wife too" he demanded.

I had to assume he didn't have breakfast money, I didn't know him that well and I wondered if he had some unfortunate things happen in his life, or whether he was just a careless spendthrift.

And I thought of the song "People need the Lord"

SCHUYLER TOOLE

It was hard for me to "dumb down" to the people in the church. Even after I explained to them that, like Isaiah, I had been called up to the Temple and given a message by God himself, people sometimes ignored me and once in a while roll their eyes when I spoke and they thought I didn't see.

But all the great ones have had to face these challenges and so I pressed on to share the vision that God shared with me and to attain the goal.

For the sake of that flock I am glad that I was there.

Eric Musgrave

I ran into Elliot Parsons at the mall. He was friendly and happy to see me and he was going on about how happy he was at his new church. He said that after his rehab he thought that a change would be good for him.

I said that I was glad to see him and wished him the best.

The problem was that his eyes were darting and he had a sort of flushed look about him. He was like a distant radio station at night that sort of fades in and out. I felt empathy for people that try to manage their hurts and problems, substance abuse or whatever. I was thinking of those who try to sweep their hurts under the rug and smile on.

For whatever reason it reminded me of the time I ran into Harley Chapman at the football game. I was there with some guys from work and we were sucking up suds and yukking it up. Harley gave me a wave.

A couple of weeks later Harley was conducting a Wednesday night seminar. He gave a little a little presentation and he wasn't quite his usual jovial self. At the end he asked if anyone in the group was dealing with any problems and trying to carry the load alone. I looked around at everybody else.

Harley stuck with it for about 5 minutes but is seemed longer. Nobody responded.

After words we had snacks and that is the only time ever that Harley was a glum, grey-faced downtrodden looking guy, except at a funeral.

JERRY YOUNGMAN

When I first started I worked in the factory. There were about 12 of us that run bench lathes. One of the guys was named Rich Lohan, he had just turned 22. He went to a different church than me and I don't think any of the other guys went to church at all.

Rich was very vocal about his faith; constantly quoting scripture to each of the guys as he thought it applied to their situation. He was scorned and openly ridiculed as we would sit around the cafeteria table at lunch or on break.

He pushed and was pushed because nobody would back him or buddy up to him. He became the butt of all the jokes. He was openly disappointed with me for not being more like him and sharing the burdens that he felt (his words)

Now that I am retired I think about guys like him once in a while. I wonder, and hope, that his faith held out and that he made it through the years and actually became an effective voice for God.

I sure hope so because I think the guy never meant any harm.

MARVIN HAWTHORNE

Today I saw a dime on the floor in the bakery section at the supermarket. I picked it up and put it in my pocket with my other change. When I got home I took my change out my pocket and put in on my night stand. That change will be used perhaps to buy a newspaper, or maybe a pack of gum.

In the same way Jesus found me; a tarnished coin tossed onto the hard concrete floor of life. He gently picked me up and placed me into one of his many pockets, sometimes called churches.

In there, along with all the other coins, I became part of his change: change to be used to present a more caring, helping person to others, and change to new hope for a future in this life and beyond.

LAVINA SIMPSON

All I have left is this night stand in this lonely prison that they call a nursing home. If only I could walk into the vestibule of that church just once more, especially at Easter. There was the special smell of the lilies, and they always looked so fine up against those light brown brick walls. O to just stand in there once more and sing one of those triumphant songs, and feel the hope again.

But those days are gone. I can only wonder what happened to Brother Boston, and to so many others who worked so hard and cared so much. But along with that comes memories of others that I cannot forget though I try.

I considered it all just routine; I took it all for granted.

But even the Bible on my nightstand says "we can never go back there", and I need to focus on where I am going, not where I have been.

Ed Carney

One year our men's softball team won the city-wide all church tournament, we got a trophy for it. I was on the team.

One Tuesday night the church board resolved that we should have a trophy case in the foyer to display it.

Soon Mrs. Winters brought in her bowling trophy and put it in the case. What an uproar! There was a very protracted legal debate about the trophy case; should it only be for church activities? The bowling league was not a church function, but she argued that she was a church member.

Finally the board voted to have her remove her trophy and she left the church in a huff. It reminded me of the time that Sharon was asked to leave the choir loft because she was wearing a silver necklace.

I will never understand how people who are supposed to be drawn together to worship the one true God can be splintered so easily. It seems to me that there are sinister forces out there that cause so much conflict and division.

I guess that what Peter meant when he described Satan as a roaring lion always looking for someone to devour.

BILLY CUNNINGHAM

A few shots (some might say gulps) of Drambuie, and I am back at the gate. The gatekeeper with his used-car-salesman smile welcomes me and lets me in. I don't think it is Satan himself, just one of his legion.

"Come on in" says he, and enjoy the scenarios here. In one, Jack Boston is just an egotistical blowhard and in another people are naïve for their criticisms of you. He goes on to tell me that my fantasies are good and I deserve those things. He says that it is unfair such things are out of my reach.

And many other scenarios present themselves, all soothing and attractive.

But at the exit gate there is no friendly face. There is only delusion followed by restless sleep and a dry throat.

Conclusion

Dusk was settling in, but earlier in the afternoon, a police officer pulled up and asked me what I was doing there. I explained who I was and why I was there. He looked me over with what I will call professional skepticism. He said "I can't tell you to leave" but he advised me to keep my doors locked and my windows up. Some children had been walking home from school, oblivious to the rich history of that abandoned, fenced off old brick structure.

Reflecting on all the faces that I had seen that afternoon, I began evaluating them one by one to determine whether they measured up. Then it occurred to me perhaps I should be more concerned about how they might think of me.

I remembered how I watched Harley Chapman lead the singing in there. He loved to do it and I always took note of his confident, peaceful smile and his swagger as he waved his hands to direct the worshippers. His favorite song was "Glory to His Name", and a lot of people called it "Down at the Cross". Although the songwriter meant it in a different context, the words "there to my heart was the blood applied" came to my mind, and that is all that remains of that place: once warm and welcoming, now eerie and forbidding.

Even so my heart cherishes the memories of that place more than words can say.

CPSIA information can be obtained
at www.ICGtesting.com
Printed in the USA
BVHW031116210120
569972BV00035B/51/J